For my brother Jerry

ONE
TEDDY LAND

When you first see the Queen of Teddy Land, you may think she is a shabby teddy bear. You may feel sorry for her and say how can a scruffy teddy bear be a Queen? But the Queen of Teddy Land was not always shabby. She had two bright eyes and was a beautiful brown bear. Then two children, Emma and Tyler Miller, cuddled and kissed her till it rubbed away her fur, and that's how she became shabby. Her name is Sylvia. She has only one eye, as the other one is lost. Sometimes the stuffing falls out of her tummy but she is the most loved bear of all the teddies in Teddy land and this is her story:

One day Sylvia wakes up in fright. She jumps out of bed and calls out 'Three days! Three days!' She rushes to the bedroom door, flings it open, hurries along the passageway and bursts into the Palace ballroom. All this hurry makes Sylvia's stuffing fall to the floor. 'No time to pick it up,' she mumbles, 'I must have a word with my brother Fred.' Fred is a slim, blue teddy bear who enjoys sitting on his throne when he eats his breakfast.

'Look at my new red trainers,' calls out Fred when he sees his sister dashing towards him.

'Never mind your trainers,' says Sylvia. 'It's been three days since the children played Teddy land.' Then she jumps high in the air and waves her paws about so that more of her stuffing tumbles to the ground.

'Don't upset yourself,' says Fred. 'You will lose too much stuffing.'

Sylvia sees the trail of fluffy stuffing lying on the floor. She bends down to pick it up and quickly pushes it back into her chest.

'Feel better now?' ask Fred.

‘No, I’m in a bad mood. I’ve a frown on my face. I must do something, or I will have this frown all day!’

‘Do some yoga then. That usually helps to get rid of frowns.’

‘You’re right, Freddie, and now I will do a handstand,’ says Sylvia and she flips over and luckily only a tiny bit more of her stuffing drops out.

‘Oh, dear, more stuffing to be picked up,’ groans Fred.

Sylvia stands on her paws looking at the ballroom upside down.

‘Turn this frown upside down. I’m upside down, but I still have a frown. Things look better upside down,’ sings Sylvia.

‘That’s the spirit,’ says Fred, munching his jam toast.

‘Fred, I have looked at Teddy Land from many directions.’

‘Yes, you have,’ answers Fred, his mouth full of jam.

‘I’ve looked high up, I’ve looked low down, from standing up, to sitting down. I’ve looked to the right; I’ve looked to the left. But it’s only today I’ve seen Teddy Land this way.’

‘What way?’ asks Fred glancing over his shoulder.

‘The day when the children stop playing Teddy Land. Who knows, it could be today?’

‘You said that yesterday. You said that the day before. You will say the same thing tomorrow.’ Fred makes a loud sound as he munches another piece of toast.

‘This is different, Fred. The children are growing up. They are not playing with teddies as they did when they were younger. Soon they will stop playing Teddy Land altogether.’ Slowly she slides down and crouches on the floor. She stands up and wanders over to the window.

‘You’re right,’ calls out Fred, ‘the children are spending more time playing computer games than playing with us.’ He wipes his paws on a serviette.

‘I thought it would change when Emma and Tyler brought home our little brother Herbert. The children love Herbert. He is a Spell and Tell bear with a computer on his phone. I thought they would play with us more, now that Herbert is here,’ says Sylvia.

‘Where is Herbert?’ Fred asks his sister, looking round the room.

‘I suppose he is in his room, as usual, playing games on his phone.’

As Sylvia wipes the window with her paws, she sees a golden bird perched on the window sill. Quickly she throws the window open, but the little bird flies away.

‘Come back, golden bird,’ calls Sylvia, But the bird has flown far away over the little houses of

Teddy Land, with their thatched roofs and brick chimneys, nestling close together. With her one good eye she can see Bluebell Woods, and further in the distance, she can make out the shape of Teddy Bear Mountain lying between Teddy Land and Dragon Land.

'They say Teddy Bear Mountain will crumble the day the children stop playing Teddy Land,' says Sylvia.

'That mountain has been here for hundreds of years,' answers Fred. 'Nothing is going to happen to our Teddy Bear Mountain.'

'I'm worried, Fred,' says Sylvia. 'Something is wrong. I've never seen a gold bird in Teddy Land before. My frown is gone but I'm still worried.'

There's a banging at the front door of the Palace.

'Did you hear that, Fred?' asks Sylvia.

'Yes,' answers Fred.

'Don't answer it,' whispers Sylvia.

KNOCK. KNOCK. KNOCK.

'We should open the door,' says Fred.

'No, I don't want to see anyone,' answers Sylvia covering her eye with a paw. 'This could be our last day in Teddy Land, and I don't want to stop playing. I will tell Sir Victor Hargreaves to open the door. We will pretend to be asleep.'

'Capital idea,' says Fred. He lets his head drop down to his chest, so it looks as if he is snoozing.

Sir Victor Hargreaves is a soft toy eagle. He has dark grey wings, a white spot on his chest, and a curved yellow beak.

'SIR VICTOR HARGREAVES!' shouts Sylvia.

'I'm in the dining room, your Majesty, polishing the silver plates.'

'Answer the door, please,' Sylvia yells back.

Bang! Bang! BANG!

'Someone needs to get the door,' shouts Sylvia.

‘Who is that someone?’ asks Sir Victor Hargreaves to himself: ‘Where is that someone? Why is that someone hearing a Bang, bang, BANG?’ Hm...I am that someone. I am Sir Victor Hargreaves polishing the silver,’ says the Eagle.

The banging at the door continues.

‘It must be me who opens the door,’ says Sir Victor Hargreaves, ‘as I am a loyal and faithful friend to Queen Sylvia.’ The eagle puffs up his soft grey chest, points his beak towards the ceiling and glides his way out of the dining room, muttering to himself.

‘Someone should get the door, but I am Sir Victor Hargreaves. I am not the butler. I am too important to be answering doors. But I suppose I am someone. But...but why is it always me?’

At that moment Sylvia comes out of the Ballroom door nearly colliding with Sir Victor Hargreaves.

‘Hargreaves?’ Sylvia whispers.

‘Yes, your Majesty.’

‘Whoever is at the door, do not let them in. Tell them I’m asleep. I don’t want to see anyone. I am going to have a big sleep. I will be asleep for five days. Bears often have five-day sleeps. A big sleep is what I need.’

Sir Victor Hargreaves skids along the slippery floor. He flies high up in the air and then swoops down to land in front of the door.

‘Let us in,’ is heard, then more shouting from behind the front door.

Sir Victor Hargreaves opens the door so quickly that something green and brown falls upon him and knocks him to the ground. ‘What’s happening?’ cries out Sir Victor Hargreaves. He looks up and sees he is lying under the tail of a green dragon, and on top of that sits a brown monkey staring down at him. The eagle shakes his wings. They are all in a tangle, the eagle, the dragon, and the monkey.

The three of them pull here and push there and at last pick themselves up. Sir Victor Hargreaves straightens his wings and stands up tall. He peers in shock at what he sees: a dragon with green wings and a light green chest and a brown monkey, very soft and furry. The monkey's chest is so shiny it looks as if she was wearing a bib.

'Who are you and why are you knocking on the Queen's door?' asks Sir Victor Hargreaves in a stern eagle voice.

'My name is Merton. I am a Zomba Dragon, and this is my daughter, Bella.'

'You can't be a Zomba Dragon. There are no Zomba dragons in Teddy Land!' proclaims Sir Victor Hargreaves.

'I think I know who I am,' replies the Zomba Dragon. 'I've lived for hundreds of years in Dragon Land. I *am* a Zomba, but there are no baby Zomba dragons anymore and that is why we adopted monkeys. We teach them to be just as magical as Zomba dragons. Isn't that right, Bella?

'Yes,' says Bella the little Zomba Monkey in her tiny voice.

'Does Zomba mean magic?' asks Sir Victor Hargreaves. 'Are both of you magical?' Sir Victor Hargreaves twitches his beak looking slightly confused.

'Yes. But never mind the chatter, I have come to see the Queen. It's most urgent,' says Merton the Zomba Dragon.

'The Queen cannot see you,' answers Sir Victor Hargreaves. 'She is fast asleep. Anyway, I am usually told if we are expecting visitors. The children, Emma and Tyler, would have told me. New toys arrive on birthdays or at Christmas or on other special occasions, but they don't arrive on their own and they never bang on doors or fall in a heap on top of me.'

'We are unusual,' says Bella the Zomba Monkey.

'This is a most unexpected turn of affairs,' says Sir Victor Hargreaves, lowering his beak and peering down at them with his piercing brown eyes.

'It is very important that we see your Queen,' repeats Merton.

'I will not allow that,' says Sir Victor Hargreaves.

'But we must see her. Tell him,' says Bella.

'Listen here, butler, we made the journey all the way from Dragon Land. There is no time to argue with you,' cries Merton.

'Butler! I am NOT the butler. I am Sir Victor Hargreaves. The loyal and faithful friend of Queen Sylvia, and this is her Palace. Everyone knows not to wake up a bear. She will be like a bear with a sore head. We must allow her to wake up in her own time.'

'But we MUST see the Queen. She is the only one who can help us!' cries Merton.

'What's all this about?' says Sir Victor Hargreaves.

'Victor, please, listen. Teddy Land is in danger. You must wake up the Queen,' pleads Merton.

'Victor?! Victor?! Nobody calls me Victor. Not even my own mother calls me Victor. I was born with this name, Sir Victor Hargreaves.'

'Please, Sir Victor Hargreaves,' begs Bella.

'What can be that urgent to make me disturb the Queen?' asks Sir Victor Hargreaves.

'Something terrible is about to happen. Teddy Bear Mountain is about to crumble and this could be the end of Teddy Land. The Queen is the only one who can save us,' says Merton.

'The mountain? Crumble? I don't like the sound of that,' says Sir Victor Hargreaves. 'Follow me, everyone, but mind the floor. It can be slippery,'

'Thank you,' says Bella and steps out only to slip and fall to the ground.'

Sir Victor Hargreaves with his bushy eyebrows stares down at Bella sprawled on the ground. 'I did warn you.'

But Bella quickly jumps up.

'I will take you to meet Sylvia, the Queen of Teddy Land.' Sir Victor Hargreaves flaps his wings as he flies along the hall. Jumping and slipping, the dragon and the monkey follow behind.

TWO
THE ZOMBA MONKEY

Queen Sylvia and her brother Fred sit on their thrones, pretending to be fast asleep. They both snore loudly. Very gently Sir Victor Hargreaves opens the door of the ballroom.

'Ahem!' says Sir Victor Hargreaves clearing his throat. Then he whispers, 'Queen Sylvia, your Majesty. Wake up please.'

Sylvia gives a loud snore. Fred yawns.

'Your Highness, you have to wake up,' says Sir Victor Hargreaves in a most tender singing voice. Sylvia opens her one eye, then quickly shuts it again.

'I know how to wake her up,' says Bella the monkey. She leaps to the ceiling and swings from the chandelier that hangs high above

Sylvia's head. The chandelier jingles as she swishes her tail.

'Bella. Get down!' cries Merton.

'But, Papa, I am trying to wake up the Queen. Wake up! Wake up, sleepy head!' yells Bella.

'Stop yelling,' yells Sir Victor Hargreaves, his wings flapping, like a windmill. 'This is NOT how you wake up a Queen!'

Fred opens one eye from his pretend sleep. Then he opens his other eye, and when he sees the monkey hanging from her tail and spinning about with the chandelier, he rubs both his eyes in surprise.

'What's going on?' Fred gasps.

Sylvia opens her one button eye and cries out, 'WHY IS A MONKEY USING MY CHANDELIER AS A SWING?'

'Stop,' calls Sir Victor Hargreaves to the monkey. She takes no notice. She dangles high and then low, holding onto the chandelier with one hand and then giving a sudden jump to catch hold of the next and all the while the glass chandelier jingles and jangles furiously.

'STOP MONKEY! STOP YOUR SWINGING RIGHT NOW!' growls Sylvia in a booming voice.

The growl is so loud that it makes Bella fall from the chandelier and land plop down, right in the middle of Sylvia's lap. The Queen stares at the little monkey. Bella jumps away and hides behind the Dragon.

'Sir Victor Hargreaves! Why have I been woken up by a monkey and a dragon? I thought I told you I was having a big sleep and was not to be woken by anyone,' growls Sylvia.

'I'm sorry, your Majesty, but there is an emergency. A Dragon has arrived and has a message for you. He says that Teddy Bear Mountain is going to crumble.'

'Apple crumble?' asks Fred.

'Biscuit crumble,' says Sylvia.

'Rhubarb crumble, I like rhubarb crumble,' laughs Fred.

'It is the Mountain, your Majesty. They say it is going to crumble,' says Sir Victor Hargreaves.

'Rubbish,' says Fred.

The dragon steps forward, making a deep bow.

'Your Majesty, my name is Merton, I am a Zomba Dragon, and I have travelled, with my daughter Bella, from far-away Dragon Land to see you.'

'Have you now?' says Sylvia as she pulls herself up from her throne and draws closer to the dragon. She peers over the dragon's tail to glare at the monkey.

'Yes, and I have come to warn you, your Majesty. Teddy Land is in danger. There is a new King in Dragon Land.

'A new King?' says Fred, standing up on his throne and looking down at the dragon.

`Yes, his name is King Rotter and he is rotten to the core, just like his name. He plans to destroy Teddy Land.'

‘Destroy Teddy Land? Nonsense!’ growls Queen Sylvia and she turns her back on the dragon and the monkey and waddles back to sit on her throne.

Bella rushes forward, The monkey jumps up and down in front of the Queen.

‘You are the Queen of Teddy Land. You are the only one who can save Teddy land.’ The monkey tugs at Sylvia’s arm trying to pull her up from her throne. Sylvia attempts to wrestle the monkey away, and in the struggle some of Sylvia’s stuffing falls out.

‘Let go of me,’ growls Sylvia.

‘You must save Teddy Land,’ squeals the monkey and lets off a wailing monkey scream.

At this moment the large doors of the Ballroom are flung open. Herbert the Spell and Tell Teddy rushes forward to help his sister.

‘Leave my sister alone, little monkey,’ shouts Herbert taking hold of the monkey and pulling her away. Herbert straightens his bow tie and dusts down his smart navy trousers.

'Herbert, oh, Herbie,' cries Sylvia. 'Thank goodness you've come. We have a dragon and a monkey who have suddenly arrived and tell us that the mountain will crumble and ...'

'Apple crumble? biscuit crumble?' asks Herbert.

'No, not apple crumble,' answers Sylvia. 'Rhubarb crumble? I don't like rhubarb crumble,' says Herbert.

'No, it has nothing to do with rhubarb crumble, Herbie. I saw a strange thing this morning. I saw a gold bird. What does a gold bird mean? Does seeing a gold bird mean the mountain will crumble? Herbie, we need information from your phone, my little brother,' says Sylvia.

Herbert removes his phone from the breast pocket of his shirt and taps the phone with his paws. He speaks into his phone: 'Is seeing a gold bird a sign that Teddy Bear Mountain is going to crumble?'

Merton interrupts, 'You saw the gold bird? We call them the butter glow birds. Yes, that is the sign that the mountain will crumble.'

'This is Merton. He says he is a Zomba Dragon. Quick, Herbert. Look him up on your Spell and Tell Phone, look up about Zomba Dragons,' demands Sylvia.

Herbert reads from his phone:

'There is only one Zomba Dragon left in Dragon Land and his name is Merton. The other Zomba dragons disappeared during the great thunder of dragons. Some people believe that there are still some Zomba dragons hiding in the mist of the mountains.'

`What about the Teddy Bear Mountain?' asks Fred.

Herbert taps some more on his phone.

'When the Teddy Bear Mountain starts to crumble, the butter glow birds fly away from the mountain. When the mountain crumbles, it is the end of Teddy land,' reads Herbert.

'Herbert, how can I believe a phone? What does a phone know?' asks Sylvia and she folds her arms in front of her chest.

'Don't like the sound of all this,' says Fred and he ties his shoelaces tighter.

'I'm just reading what it says on my phone, Freddy,' replies Herbert.

Warning, warning. Red light, red light. Suddenly Herbert's phone speaks in an unusual robotic voice.

'What is your phone doing now, Herby?' asks Sylvia.

'I don't know, sister. It looks like it's printing something.'

The Spell and Tell Phone makes a creaking sound as it prints out small pieces of paper. More and more paper notes pour out of the phone and float about the room. The pieces stick to Herbert's brown fur and cover his eyes.

'Help! Get them off me!' says Herbert in a

muffled voice. Bella hurries to pick the notes from Herbert's fur. Notes fly about and the teddies run to pick them up.

Two pieces of paper cover Herbert's eyes. He pulls them off and looks around.

'Sylvia, Sylvia, you are the Queen. Do something,' shouts Bella as she jumps up again to cling to the chandelier.

'Silence,' growls Sylvia in such a deep voice that the monkey and the chandelier drop to the floor and the glass smashes.

'Everyone, stop talking. I need to think. We need to come up with a plan,' says Sylvia.

The Teddies pace up and down the room. They walk around the monkey, being careful not to tread on the broken chandelier on the floor.

'I've got it. I have a plan. I think we should go to the mud pool and visit Walter the Hippo and his family. The Hippos know about Teddy Bear Mountain. They will help us,' says Sylvia.

'Yes, my sister, what a good idea. Let us go

to the mud pool and ask the Hippos to advise us,' says Fred.

Queen Sylvia dashes out of the Throne Room and immediately Fred, Herbert, Sir Victor Hargreaves, Merton, and Bella rush after her.

THREE

THE MONSTER OF THE MOUNTAIN

In the deepest and darkest part of Dragon Land, in a castle covered with slimy green leaves lives the blue dragon, King Rotter. On the walls of his castle hang paintings of his ancestors. These are large pictures of his grandparents, his great aunts, his great uncles, and all the rest of his ancient ancestors. Wherever he walks, their googly eyes and squishy faces follow him.

'Be strong, Rotter. You are the King now and you must rule your kingdom as we have done before.' Their voices echo through the great halls and along the long corridors. King Rotter answers them.

'Yes, Grandfather and Grandmother Rotter,

I wear the silver crown of Dragon Land now. I will not let you down.'

King Rotter hears snuffling and snoring coming from the big hall. He hurries to check that his two dragon guards are doing their job. 'ARE YOU ASLEEP?' shouts King Rotter. 'No, your Highness, we're awake,' murmur Teeth, the purple dragon, and Yella, the yellow dragon, jumping to their feet, their voices shaking as they rub their sleepy eyes. 'No, not the two of you! I mean the Monster Narodoon. That red monster over there, lying fast asleep on my dining room table. Look at her! Isn't she fantastic?'

'Yes, Your Highness, she is fantastic,' answered the two guards.

'She is a wonderful creature, and your Highness did the most brave thing!' Yella says, 'You woke up the Monster of Teddy Bear Mountain.'

'I did,' smiled King Rotter. 'It was me, only

me.'

'You did what other dragons never dared to do,' says Teeth, in a deep throaty voice.

'Yes, I proved them wrong. I woke up the Monster of the Mountain and I, the great King Rotter, dragged the Monster Narodoon to my castle.'

'I don't like the look of her slimy tail,' says Teeth.

'She has a mouth at the end of her tail,' says Yella. 'And that mouth tried to bite me.'

'She tried to bite you because you woke her up,' says Teeth.

'I was only following the orders from our King,' says Yella.

'Guards, guards, stop squabbling. You did good work. Now do as I say. Wake her up,' bellows King Rotter.

'But how do I wake her up?' asks Yella, his knees wobbling.

'Poke her with a stick,' says Teeth.

'A stick! We don't have sticks lying around. This is a castle, not a forest,' says King Rotter. 'Here, try with this fork.' King Rotter picks up a fork from the table.

Teeth grabs the fork and pokes Narodoon's tail.

Narodoon's mouth at the end of her tail opens wide and makes a hissing sound like a snake. She leaps into the air. Her tail whips, slashes and slices the air. The walls tremble, the paintings rattle and the ceiling creaks. This makes Teeth drop the fork in fright.

'Yeeeks!' screams Teeth.

'Yeeks!' screams Narodoon.

'You should have poked her with a stick,' mumbles Yella as he scurries into a corner to hide.

'That hurt,' says Narodoon.

'We had to wake you,' says King Rotter.

'You woke me up with a spell, when I was deep asleep in the mountain. Now you woke me up again and now I know what I want to be. I want to be a real monster and leave the Make believe of Teddy Worlds. I want to go for walks along the bank of the river, swim in the lake, and dive through waves in the sea,' cries Narodoon, waving her great feet in the air.

'GOOD IDEA!' shouts King Rotter. 'I want to be a real Dragon too! I want to leave Dragon Land and enter the real world and be a real dragon. I'm fed up with the way the children fuss over the teddy bears and pay more attention to them than to me. After all, I am important. I am King Rotter of Dragon Land. Why don't they love me? It's that Sylvia, why do they keep saying she is the Queen of Teddy land?'

'I know how to make you a real Dragon!' says Narodoon, 'but I need the Book of Zomba.'

'The Book of Zomba has been stolen,' answers King Rotter.

'WHAT'S THAT YOU SAY?' shouts Narodoon as she breathes fire from her nose.

'The Zomba Dragon Merton took it,' says King Rotter his eyes flashing with anger. 'He ripped it from me, but I was too clever for him. I tore off this page and I have it here.' King Rotter lifts his left wing and shows Narodoon a piece of torn paper.

Narodoon jumps forward and with her claws grabs the paper and then flattens it out using her tail.

'Only one page! This is not enough. I must have the book. The book has the whole spell. The spell that will turn us into real dragons!' says Narodoon swishing her tail again, crashing it hard on the stone floor.

Teeth and Yella stamp their feet in agreement.

Narodoon snorts and cries and through her red nostrils makes bursts of fire fill the air.

'I am the Great Narodoon. I have been asleep inside Teddy Bear Mountain for many years, but now I'm awake at last. I vow to turn myself into a real monster.'

'We must get the book. The book of Wisdom,' chimes King Rotter.

'Good idea,' says the Monster Narodeen. 'You are a rotter and know about doing rotten things.'

'I am and thank you for the compliment.'

'Let's go for it! Let's begin,' shouts Narodoon.

'LET THE MOUNTAIN CRUMBLE. LET THE MOUNTAIN CRUMBLE!' says King Rotter.

Narodoon breathes on the piece of paper that was torn from the Book of Wisdom. The piece of paper becomes a mirror. 'Now we can spy on the Teddies with this mirror,' says Narodoon. 'Now we can see if the teddies have got the Book of Wisdom.'

King Rotter and the monster Narodoon turn to the guards and in one voice says,

'Now, Teeth and Yella. You are to do a very important job. You must watch the mirror and spy all night and day on Sylvia, and her friends and family.'

Teeth and Yella stand to attention and say,

'We're the guards. You can rely on the two of us to keep her under surveillance.'

'What is she up to now?' cries King Rotter, greatly excited.

They all look closely at the mirror.

'I see,' says Narodoon, 'that Sylvia is trudging towards the Mud pool at the foot of Teddy Bear Mountain.'

'Yes, she is with Merton, the Zomba Dragon and some others,' says King Rotter.

King Rotter flings his tail above his head and cries out, 'The book –the Book of Wisdom. The book of Zomba. That dragon Merton has it! He must be stopped."

'Let's go,' cries Narodoon.

'Get the book!'

'Get the Zomba Dragon.'

King Rotter leads the way. They all dash to the window. The window is thrown open.

Narodoon, Teeth, and Yella follow King Rotter as he flies across the sky towards Teddy Land.

'GO. GO. GO!'

FOUR
THE HIP TO THE HOP

Queen Sylvia sees her friend Walter, the purple hippo, splashing about in the mud pool. What fun to play in the mud with your little hippo family, she thinks. I wish I could play in the cool water like that. I wish I didn't have to worry about the crumbling mountain.

'Sylvia! Come and join my family in this squelchy mud bath. It's so lovely on the skin,' calls Walter.

'I can't,' she answers sadly. 'There's trouble in Teddy Land. A Zomba dragon and a Zomba monkey have brought bad news. The mountain is going to crumble. They say it could be the end of Teddy Land.'

'What's that?'

‘Yes, and only a loved, shabby bear, a Queen, like me, can save Teddy Land.’

‘REALLY?’ he bellows back.

‘YES,’ she shouts, ‘they say the mountain will crumble.’

‘What kind of crumble? apple crumble? Rhubarb crumble?’ calls back Walter.

‘Oh, don’t start with the crumble again,’ says Sir Victor Hargreaves in his usual snooty voice.

‘Nonsense. Don’t worry. The mountain has been here for hundreds of years. Have a mud bath,’ says Walter cheerily.

‘There’s no time for mud baths,’ says Merton the dragon.

‘Who’s that?’ says Walter as he rolls some more in the muddy water.

‘I am Merton, and this is my daughter Bella, the Zomba monkey.’

‘Hello to you,’ says Walter. ‘Meet my wife, Angela, and our son Pinkie.’

‘Hellooooo,’ calls Angela, a pink hippo,

diving into the pool and splashing some mud on Merton and Bella.

'Sorry. I didn't mean to splash you with mud. I was trying out a new dive,' says Angela.

Walter notices his son Pinkie about to throw more mud on Merton and Bella. 'PINKIE!' cries Walter. 'Stop throwing mud right now.'

Pinkie stops and Herbert looks relieved as he brushes some of the splatters off his white clean shirt.

'This is my daughter, Kim,' Walter says, pointing to a silver hippo who is swimming in the pool. Queen Sylvia slumps down on the grassy bank.

'Cheer up, Sylvia, my daughter will sing you a song and we can all do a hippo dance. That will cheer you up,' says Walter.

Kim jumps out of the pool and begins to dance on a little wooden stage next to the mud pool.

'Who put the Hip in the Hop? Who put the

Hop in the Hip?' sings Kim.

'Hippo did!' sings Walter the Hippo.

All the Teddies start to dance and clap their hands.

'Put your hands on your hips and do the Hip, Hip, Hop, Hippo dance. Who put the Hip in the Hop? Who put the Hop in the Hip? Hippos did. It's Hippo Hop. Do the Hippo bop, Hippo Hip, Hippo Hop. Do the Hippo bop, to the Hippo Hop.'

Walter, Angela and their kids, Pinkie and Kim, dance and hop together. Soon the teddies join in. They hop on one leg and join in with the singing.

'And hop on one leg and do the Hippo Hop. Who put the Hip in the Hop? Hippos did!' all the Hippos sing.

'We put the 'po' in the Hippo,' sings Walter in a low voice.

'Who put the Hip in the Hop?' sings Angela.

'Hippos did,' responds Pinkie.

‘Who put the ‘po’ in the Hippo,’ Walter repeats in his low voice.

Hopping on one leg to the Hippo Bop, Queen Sylvia says, ‘I feel so much better.’

‘Please, Sylvia. Stop dancing,’ says Sir Victor Hargreaves. ‘We are running out of time. We need to save Teddy Land.’

‘Have a hip, have a hop. Do the Hippo bop,’ sings Sylvia.

‘The dragons will be coming. We are not safe. They are coming. They are coming,’ says Bella.

‘It’s so catchy. Who put the Hip in the Hop?’ sings Fred.

‘Hippos did!’ sings Sylvia, as she hops on one leg and puts her hands on her hips.

‘We need to save Teddy Bear Mountain. Save Teddy Land,’ says Bella and she starts to pull at Sylvia’s arm. ‘Queen Sylvia, we should listen to the dragon. Stop the dancing...’ Sir Victor Hargreaves says.

‘Who put the Hip in the Hop?’ Sylvia sings quietly to herself.

‘The mountain!’ exclaims Sir Victor Hargreaves.

The teddies continue to dance.

‘They are not listening,’ says Sir Victor Hargreaves to Bella.

A dark shadow covers the mud pool. A cold breeze rustles in the trees.

‘Look! A shadow! It’s the dragons; they are coming!’ shrieks Bella.

‘Hide me!’ yells Merton.

Bella waves her hand over Merton’s face and slowly her magic makes him disappear.

‘Dragons in the sky, Sylvia!’ shouts Sir Victor Hargreaves.

The hippo and the teddies stop their dancing. They see four dragons flying towards them and behind them is Narodoon.

“It’s a monster. They have woken up the monster of the mountain. Hippos back in the mud pool,' says Walter.

The hippo family dive into the mud pool.

Teeth, the purple dragon, flies low and Yella, the yellow dragon, comes swooping down onto the mud pool and, with his large claws, he picks up Pinkie.

'Help!' calls out Pinkie. The dragon drops Pinkie into the mud pool.

'Hey, that was fun!' says Pinkie. Suddenly the ground shakes. A thunderous roar fills the air. The sound of Narodoon's tail thrashes through the reeds. A shadow covers the teddies.

'Where is she?' bellows Narodoon's voice.

"Where is your Queen?' repeats the second voice from the end of Naradoon's tail. Then both mouths blow fire that fills the air with smoke. King Rotter flies through the smoke and down he crashes landing in the mud pool.

'Teddies! The monster of the Mountain, the Great Narodoon, wants to talk to your Queen Sylvia' demands King Rotter.

‘Here I am,’ announces Sylvia.

Narodoon lands in a flash, next to Sylvia. `AND HERE I AM NARODOON. Be warned. I am awake and soon the mountain will fall. No child will ever play Teddy Land again. We will come back and steal all the little teddies from Teddy Land because we know you have the Zomba dragon and the Book of Zomba,’ threatens Narodoon.

‘What Zomba dragon? What Book of Zomba? I don’t know what you are talking about?’ says Sylvia, in a sweet voice.

‘I don’t believe you. You’re just trying to protect him. I will destroy Teddy Land,’ shouts Narodoon and she shakes her long body blowing out a huge ball of fire from her two mouths.

FIVE

THE TEDDY BEAR MEETING.

'How dare you lie?' cries the two mouths belonging to Narodoon, the Monster of the Mountain, as she stamps around the Teddy Queen.

'Oh, that Zomba dragon? He vanished when we were singing the Hippo song,' replies Sylvia, not sure where to look. Should she speak to Narodoon's tail or her face?

'I don't care about your fibs. I don't care about Hippo songs. You listen to me. When he comes back, you must bring him to me.'

Then Narodoon sees Bella the Zomba monkey with Herbert hiding behind a bush. Narodoon stumbles forward trying to grab

Herbert, but Bella pulls him and they both vanish.

Narodoon licks her sharp teeth in anger. 'These Zomba monkeys are too quick for me,' complains Narodoon.

'Too quick,' repeats the mouth at the end of her tail.

'Stop repeating everything I say,' says Narodoon to her tail.

Her tail repeats, 'Stop repeating everything I say.'

Queen Sylvia says: 'I haven't said anything.'

'I was speaking to my tail,' says Narodoon.

'I thought you wanted to speak to me.'

'I do,' replies Narodoon. 'Why do you teddies get me in a muddle? Now listen to this.'

King Rotter sweeps down and snatches up Fred, Pinkie and Kim in his claws.

'Be warned, Queen Sylvia,' says Narodoon. 'Bring me the Zomba dragon before sunset or we will be back to take more of the teddies away.' With that, Narodoon spreads her wings and flies off with King Rotter and the other dragons to Dragon Land.

'Help! My darlings! My children! The dragons have got my Kim and Pinkie!' cries Angela.

'Fred! They have my brother Fred!' shouts Sylvia.

'Your majesty. This is an emergency. We need to hold a Teddy Bear meeting.' says Sir Victor Hargreaves.

'Yes, a Teddy Bear meeting,' says Sylvia, with a wobble in her voice.

'I will fly over Teddy Land and call everyone to come to your Palace,' says Sir Victor Hargreaves.

'They took my babies away,' sobs Angela.

'My Little Hippos,' moans Walter as he puts his arm around her.

There is a flash of blue light and Bella, Merton and Herbert reappear. Sylvia throws her arms around her brother Herbert and hugs him. 'The dragons have taken Fred, Kim and Pinkie,' weeps Sylvia.

'We saw it all. We were invisible but we watched everything,' says Merton.

Queen Sylvia gives the command for them all to return to the Palace for the Teddy Bear meeting.

Back in the Palace, the teddies charge into the Ballroom, chattering and calling to each other. Queen Sylvia hurries to her throne.

'Silence!' cries Sylvia. 'Merton, the Zomba dragon, wants to speak.'

Merton with his green tail swishing behind him steps slowly forward. 'Teddies, I need to tell you about the mysteries of the mountain. Narodoon who you know is half monster, half dragon is the one who guards the secret key of the land of Make believe. King Rotter has woken up Narodoon and the key has disappeared.

There is a silence in the room. Then everyone

calls out.

'What? What? The key is lost. What will happen now?' cry out the teddies. 'To save Teddy Land we have to find the key.' Bella jumps onto the piano.

'I told you! I told you! Teddy Land is in danger,' screeches Bella as she stamps on the piano keys.

'We must find the key. It's the only way to save Fred, the hippo children and to save Teddy Land,' says Merton.

'What does the key look like?' asks Sylvia.

'It's a gold key with a butter glow bird engraved on it.' replies Merton.

'We have to go to Dragon Land to get back Fred,' says Sylvia.

'No, this is the only way you will be able to get back Fred, you have to find the key,' says Merton.

'We will find the key to open the door to the land of Make believe,' says Herbert

‘Where is this door?’ shouts Walter in his gruff hippo voice.

‘Door? I open the doors for Her Majesty. That’s my job,’ says Sir Victor Hargreaves.

‘Yes, you’re the butler,’ says Walter.

‘Walter, I am not the butler. I am Sir Victor Hargreaves, loyal and faithful friend to the Queen.’

‘Silence, everyone,’ says the Queen. ‘We are talking about the door to the land of Make believe.’

‘I’m confused,’ says Angela. ‘Keys, doors, the monster being woken up and what about Fred, Pinkie and Kim?’

‘I promise you will get them back when we find the key,’ says Merton.

‘Do you know where we can find the key?’ asks Herbert.

‘I have seen a key in a door,’ says the Queen. ‘We must leave Teddy Land and go to our playroom. Go back to our children Emma and

Tyler. That is where I have seen a key.'

'Should I make some sandwiches?' asks Angela.

'It will be a long journey,' says her husband, Walter.

'Right. Five minutes to get ready,' says Queen Sylvia `Meet me outside Walter's house. Angela will supply packed lunches.'

The teddies rush home to get what they need to leave Teddy Land. The floor is slippery and the teddies skid out of the Palace. Queen Sylvia spins out of the door and into the front garden. In the Ballroom, Walter rushes to the piano.

'You don't need the piano,' says Bella as she jumps up and down on the keys.

'Hippos have to have music,' replies Walter and he pushes and shoves the piano through the front door, squashing Sir Victor Hargreaves against the door frame.

'Take a smaller instrument with you,' squawks

Sir Victor Hargreaves, his beak flattened against the piano keys.

Walter gives the piano one big push and the piano breaks into two pieces. Sir Victor Hargreaves, Bella the monkey and the piano keys fly through the air. 'I will just bring my tin whistle,' says Walter.

Sir Victor Hargreaves, who has fallen through the air with the piano, lands on the soft grass. Sylvia, dizzy with the hurry, staggers over to sit beside him. 'I do hope we can find the key. We must save Fred and the Hippos,' says Queen Sylvia as she rubs his sore beak. A rumbling sound echoes through Teddy Land. Large rocks and upturned bushes tumble down from the top of Teddy Bear Mountain.

SIX
ROCK CAKES AND CRUMBLE.

Walter and his hippo family live in an old stone cottage. The house is very run down. Hippos are not very good at keeping a tidy house. The garden fence is broken, the tiles on the roof are cracked, and in the front garden, there is a broken trampoline with a big hippo hole in it.

The Teddies are waiting outside the Hippos' house. 'Where are you, Hippos? Walter! Angela! We will leave without you. Hurry up!' shouts Sylvia. Angela runs out of the house carrying two big picnic baskets. 'Wait for us,' she says, huffing and puffing. Walter rushes out and slams the door shut.

'Watch out, Walter,' shouts Sylvia. Walter

looks up at the mountain. He sees a large rock hurtling towards him. Quickly, he jumps out of the way. The rock lands on the broken fence, just missing Herbert.

'Hailstones!' shrieks Herbert.

'They're not hailstones; they're rocks from the mountain,' says Angela.

'Ouch, that hit me on the leg,' Herbert yelps.

'It's dangerous here with all these flying rocks. We better go to Bluebell Woods for safety,' says Sylvia as she runs down the lane, dodging the rocks.

The teddies run after Sylvia. More rocks fall from the sky. Merton the dragon calls out as he flies over the teddies.

'This is far as we can go. Sylvia, you must find the key. We will come back when you need us,' says Merton the Dragon. Merton flaps his wings, and with Bella the monkey on his back, he glides into the air.

'But when will we see you again?' calls out

Sylvia. But they are gone. Sylvia stands and faces the teddies. 'Now that we are in Bluebell woods, let's return to the Playroom in Frog Water Hill. To do this you must follow my actions,' says Sylvia. 'Touch your knees, rub your head, rub your tummy, wave your arms, touch your nose, and reach for your paws, open a door. Step forward and let the magic start. Let us return from Teddy Land to Frog Water Hill,' says Sylvia.

Sylvia's fur begins to sparkle. The Teddies spin and as they spin Teddy Land disappears. Then the spinning stops and they are back in the playroom.

'We are back. I love the playroom with the paintings of bluebells and gold birds on the walls,' says Sylvia.

'I love the train set on the floor,' says Herbert.

'A rocking horse,' says Sir Victor Hargreaves

'A doll's house,' says Angela.

'A window seat,' says Walter.

‘Where are the children? Where are Emma and Tyler? They should be in the playroom?’ Sylvia asks.

‘They’re not here,’ replies Angela.

‘Come on,” says Sir Victor Hargreaves, ‘we must find the key.’

‘Follow me,’ says Sylvia.

The Teddies arrive at the door to the attic. A metal key is sticking out of the lock, high up.

‘I can’t reach the key,’ Herbert shouts.

‘Lift me up. I will get the key,’ orders Sir Victor Hargreaves.

Sir Victor Hargreaves climbs up on the teddies, and with his beak, he turns the key. The door swings open. All the teddies fall to the ground. Sir Victor Hargreaves with the key in his beak also falls. Sylvia takes the key from his beak and looks at the key. ‘This is not the key. Look, It is the attic, I need to go into the attic and find the right key,’ says Sylvia.

‘But what is behind the door? What is the

attic?' asks Angela

'It is a room in a house under the roof. A place where lost things go like the key.' answers Herbert.

Bravely, Queen Sylvia strides into the pitch-black attic. She bumps into a box, hurts her paw, then stumbling forward hurts her other paw on a second box. 'OW!'

'Are you alright?' asks a voice behind her.

'Who's that?' says Sylvia.

'It's me. Herbert.'

Sylvia sees a ray of light coming from the doorway and there's Herbert standing with all the other teddies. 'Herbie, I can't see properly. It's too dark.'

'I've a torch on my phone,' says Herbert. 'That'll help.'

'As your loyal faithful friend, I believe I should come as well,' says Sir Victor Hargreaves.

The door of the attic closes behind them. 'Shine the torch over there, Herbert,' says Sir

Victor Hargreaves. Sylvia peers into a nearby box. 'Look at this, china cups wrapped up in old newspaper.' Herbert shines the light inside the box. 'W-w-w-what's that noise?' stutters Herbert. 'It's coming from behind those boxes,' says Sylvia.

Herbert shines the torch again. 'It looks like a brown Teddy Bear!' says Sylvia in surprise.

'Help me. I am stuck!' shouts the brown Teddy.

'I am coming,' answers Sylvia as she takes hold of the teddy bear's arm and gives a gentle pull. Dust flies into the air. All the teddies cough. Sylvia pulls the brown teddy bear until she is free.

Sylvia stares at the brown teddy bear. She wipes away dust from the teddy bear's fur.

'You look like me,' says Sylvia.

'You look like me,' answers the dusty, brown teddy bear. 'But you are dusty,' says Sylvia.

'That's my name. Dusty.' She brushes away

more dust from her fur.' My name is Sylvia,' she says.

'I know your name. I've heard the children talk about you,' answers Dusty. 'We must be sisters, I have been lost in the attic and you are my long lost sister,' says Dusty.

'I didn't know I had a sister,' says Sylvia.

'Do you think we were made in the same toy shop?' asks Dusty.

'Were you made by the toy maker Mama May? In a toy shop in Copenhagen?' asks Sylvia.

'Yes, I come from the toy shop in Copenhagen,' replies Dusty.

'Me too! So, you *are* my sister,' exclaims Sylvia with delight. 'Let me give you a big hug. Come and meet our little brother, Herbert.'

'Your Majesty, may I do the introductions? I am Sir Victor Hargreaves. Loyal and faithful friend to Queen Sylvia of Teddy Land.'

'We have not got time for introductions, Sir Victor Hargreaves. We must find the key,' says

Sylvia.

'What are you looking for?' asks Dusty.

'I am looking for the key to Make believe.'

'Why?'

'Because Teddy Land is in danger. The dragons have captured our brother Fred, and we must save him. Teddy Bear Mountain is crumbling. Unless we find the key the children will never play Teddy Land again,' says Sylvia.

'Oh, no,' says Dusty. 'We must save Teddy Land. I'm glad I have found my family because now I can help you find the key.'

SEVEN
HELP! HELP!

'The question is where are we to find the key in this attic so full of boxes and other things?' asks Sir Victor Hargreaves.

Dusty replies 'We can ask the two scarecrows, Chit Chat and Scarecrowie, they will know. They happen to be staying in a suitcase over in that corner but most of the time they are suitcase hoppers. They travel the world in different suitcases.'

Dusty skips to their suitcase and opens it. 'Wake up, Scarecrowie. Wake up, Chit Chat. My sister wants your help.'

Chit Chat and Scarecrowie jump out of the suitcase and shake the dust from their sparkly hats.

'Make hay while the sun shines,' calls out Scarecrowie, looking at Queen Sylvia.

'Hay- day! Hay-day!' shout the two scarecrow toys, dancing about on their suitcase.

'Is this true? The famous Queen of Teddy Land has come to our attic?'

'Yes, here I am, and I need you to help me find the key to Make believe,' says Sylvia.

'We can help you. We travel around the world hopping from airport to airport. We've seen a lot from suitcases. But there are thousands of keys in the world. How will we know which one?'

'I have been told that it is a gold key, with a gold bird engraved in it,' replies Sylvia.

'I think I may have something that will help us,' says Scarecrowie and he scurries back into the suitcase only to return moments later holding a leaflet in his hand.

'We collect tourist information, leaflets, and maps of cities on our travels. This leaflet is about the Tower of London,' he says. Scarecrowie reads the leaflet aloud: 'Every night during the ceremony of keys the Tower of London is locked up. It happens at seven minutes to ten o'clock.

'At 21:53 pm to be exact,' interrupts Herbert.

'I know that in the Tower of London there are nine ravens. They are very big birds,' says Chit Chat.

'Let me tell you about the Chief Yeoman Warder,' says Scarecrowie

'Who is the Chief Yeoman Warder? Is he a raven?' asks Chit Chat.

'No, he is not a raven. Forget about the ravens. He is a guard who locks the doors of the Tower of London,' explains Scarecrowie.

'How can I forget about ravens? I am a scarecrow. I think about birds all the time,' says Chit Chat as he tries to grab the leaflet off Scarecrowie.

Sylvia and Herbert look at the leaflet.

'Here's a picture of the Chief Yeoman

Warder. He is holding a lantern and keys,' says Herbert.

'Yes, look at that key, the one on the left. Is that the right key?' Sylvia asks. Sir Victor Hargreaves draws nearer to have a look.

'It looks like the key to Make believe?' he says.

'Come on then Sir Victor Hargreaves. Let's go to the Tower of London and get the key.' Herbert tries to open the door of the attic, but it won't budge. 'I can't open it.' Herbert stutters.

'Let me try,' says Scarecrowie. Both the Scarecrows try to open the door.

'Help! Let us out!' calls out Herbert.

`What are we going to do?' Sylvia says, shaking her arms about. 'We need to be on time for the ceremony of keys.'

'Help!' calls Herbert and he bangs hard on the door.

EIGHT
THE BOOK OF ZOMBA.

Now back in Dragon Land, Narodoon, King Rotter, and two guard dragons study the mirror. They can see a picture of Queen Sylvia in the attic.

'Look, the Queen is trapped in the attic,' cackles Narodoon as she holds the mirror.

'Very good,' says King Rotter, swishing his tail. Then he turns to his prisoners, Fred and the two hippos, Kim and Pinkie.

'We want to go home,' squeal the hippos sadly,

'Stop your whining. You hippos and Fred listen to me. Your sister will never get the key from the Tower of London, and soon the mountain will crumble.'

'My sister Sylvia will rescue us,' shouts Fred in a loud, brave voice.

'Why did we have to kidnap hippos?' says King Rotter. "They are very annoying, crying like babies. We should have taken Herbert with his phone. In fact, I've have sent my dragons to the playroom to capture Sylvia's little brother Herbert and bring him to Dragon land. Then I can smash his phone and he won't be so clever,' says King Rotter.

'Good idea, and I will send two butter glow birds to the Tower of London to get the key,' says Narodoon.

She gives a long whistle to call the two butter glow birds. They fly through the open window, into dragon castle. 'butter glow birds, go and fetch the key to Make believe. It is in the Tower of London, bring it to me,' orders Narodoon.

Fred yells, 'Our Sylvia will get the key!'

'Are you still talking?' snarls King Rotter. 'I

think it's time we took Fred and the hippos to Teddy Bear Mountain and tie them up. That will keep them quiet. When the mountain crumbles, they will be crushed. The mountain will fall, and their Queen Sylvia won't be able to save them. Teeth, take them away,' orders King Rotter.

The purple dragon flies towards the hippos and with his sharp teeth, he lifts them up into the air and flies out of the open window.

The other dragons follow.

In the attic Sylvia and the teddies thump on the closed door.

'Help!' calls out Sir Victor Hargreaves in a croaky voice.

'It's no good. No one is coming, We have been stuck in this attic for hours' says Sylvia. 'What time is it?'

'8:30 pm,' replies Herbert.

'If only Walter and Angela came to find us,' says Sylvia.

'Don't worry. They'll find us, they know

where we are,' says Herbert.

'We have an hour and twenty three minutes to get to the Tower. We must be at the ceremony of keys by 9:53 pm,' says Sir Victor Hargreaves.

'My phone doesn't work. It's in spelling mode. What will we do? We could be stuck in the attic forever?' wails Herbert.

'Spell forever. F-O-R-E-V-E-R,' says the phone.

'No,' growls Sylvia and she picks up a china teacup to throw it.

'Queen Sylvia, put down that cup!' calls out Sir Victor Hargreaves.

'No! I am not going to smash this cup.' says Sylvia as she throws herself onto the floor, lies on her back and kicks her paws in the air. 'How are we going to get out of this attic? It makes me angry being stuck in here.' Dusty pats Sylvia's arm and removes the china cup from her.

'Sometimes you need to look at a problem in a different way.' Dusty strokes her sister's furry face. 'We can come up with an answer. You don't need to growl or smash things. You just need to think and try to solve the problem,' says Dusty.

Sylvia stares at the roof and says,

'I can see a window up there.'

'That's an idea,' says Dusty. 'We could climb out of the window. The window doesn't open all the way, but it opens enough for teddies to squeeze out. We could climb onto the roof and slide down the chimney. Then we can go down into the playroom.'

'I'm not climbing onto the roof,' says Sylvia.

'Her Majesty has a fear of heights, ever since she lost her eye,' says Sir Victor Hargreaves.

'How did you lose your eye?' asks Dusty.

'Maybe a bird took your eye,' says Chit Chat.

'We have no time for a chit chat about my eye. We need a plan, I will make myself climb the roof,' says Sylvia.

'We can use Chesney, the hobby horse,' says

Dusty. ‘We can hold onto his stick and climb together.’

‘The hobby horse?’ asks Sylvia.

‘Yes, he’s fast asleep in the corner. I will wake him up. Chesney. ...Chesney. We need your help,’ says Dusty.

‘Neigh, neigh, what is it?’ says Chesney the hobby horse with his eyes half open, sleepily.

‘We are locked in the attic. We need you to help us climb onto the roof so we can slide down the chimney,’ pleads Dusty.

‘Ok, I will show you and your friends how to climb onto the roof. I have done it before,’ says the hobby horse.

The hobby horse wobbles and then bounces over to the window. The horse pushes the window open and then sticks his head out of it. ‘Quick, everyone. Get hold of his stick and he can pull us up,’ says Chit Chat as he grabs hold of the hobby horse’s stick. The teddies cling to the hobby horse. The horse slowly moves along the roof and the teddies hold on. Sylvia keeps her eye firmly shut.

Then they all climb off the hobby horse to sit on top of the roof.

'Look at the view,' says Dusty.

'I don't want to look,' says Sylvia.

'Open your eye, you'll be ok. I have your paw,' says Dusty as she holds her sister's paw.

Sylvia opens her eye. 'Wow, I can see over London from here,' says Sylvia.

'See those buildings over there? That's where we need to go. We need to go, to the Tower of London,' says Herbert.

'Come on then,' says Sylvia as she slides down the chimney.

The Teddies scream as they fall down the chimney. Thick black dust covers them as they land with a bump in the playroom. The Teddies fall one on top of the other and roll onto the floor. They are covered with dust.

Walter and Angela come rushing over to

the Teddies.

'I was calling you from the attic,' cries Sylvia to Walter and Angela. 'Why didn't you hear me?'

'It was the dragons. We had to hide in the playroom,' Walter and Angela replied together.

'Dragons? It is not safe here. I want to go back to the attic,' says a scared Scarecrowie.

'Are you okay?' asks Walter.

'Yes, and we know where we can find the key,' Sylvia declares.

'My phone says the quickest way is to travel by train. We need to get the London Underground. Then take the northern line from Highgate station to London Bridge' says Herbert.

'Well, let's do that then,' says Sylvia, as a dark shadow covers her face. Herbert grabs Sylvia's arm.

Then there's a shouting and crying out.

'Dragons! Hide, everyone. Hide in the playroom again!' shouts Walter.

A shadow covers the walls of the hallway. Several green and purple dragons fly toward the teddies.

The teddies run and scatter into the playroom, hiding under chairs, blankets, and cushions.

'I can form a dust ball, stand close to me,' yells Dusty as she makes a large ball of dust. Sylvia, Herbert, and a few other teddies are huddled close to Dusty as she forms a cloud of dust to cover them. The dragons swoop low and grab Angela by the legs. She tries to climb up the curtains. Another dragon snatches Walter with his claws. The dragons grab Scarecrowie. They pick up Chesney the hobby horse by his stick as he gallops around the room. 'Leave me alone. I have nothing to do with them,' shrieks Chesney as the dragons pull the stick of the hobby horse by his teeth.

Meanwhile, the dustball gets bigger and bigger. 'DUSTBALLS!' Dusty calls out.

The dragons start to cough. 'Too dusty!' roars one of the dragons. Another dragon lets out a large fiery sneeze. 'Where's Queen Sylvia. She is in that dustball! Get her! Get Herbert.' howls one of the Dragons. 'The dust is hurting my eyes,' growls another dragon.

'Come on. Let's go,' snarls the purple dragon who appears to be the leader, and with that, the dragons fly off with the teddies. The dust falls to the ground and Sylvia, Dusty, Herbert, Sir Victor Hargreaves, and Chit Chat are left lying on the floor.

The five teddies sit up. 'They took Walter and Angela,' yells Sylvia in distress. 'They took my brother, Scarecrowie!' cries Chit Chat. 'This is too dangerous. I have to go to the Tower of London on my own and find the key myself,' says Sylvia.

'You can't go on your own. They have ravens in the Tower of London and I am a scarecrow. Scarecrows can talk to the ravens so I should come with you,' says Chit Chat.

Sir Victor Hargreaves injects, 'I am a bird so if anyone can talk to ravens it is me. I will always be by your side, my Queen, to offer my services.

'I can hide us in the shadows of a dust ball,' says Dusty.

'Don't forget, I have the phone and can use the map to show us the way to the Tower of London,' says Herbert.

'Okay, come with me,' says Sylvia. 'We need to save Teddy Land,' and she leads the way out of the playroom.

NINE
FROG WATER HILL.

They creep down the stairs and make their way to the cat flap in the kitchen. The teddies climb out of the cat flap one by one. Chit Chat pushes Dusty out of the cat flap and, as he does, dust fills the air. Chit Chat tries to hold onto a sneeze as he does not want to wake up the dog that is sleeping in his basket, but the dust is too much for him and he sneezes. The dog wakes up.

'Quick! The dog is awake,' yelps Chit Chat as he jumps out of the cat flap.

The teddies run along the garden path and onto the main road. The dog barks after them.

Chit Chat, Dusty, Sir Victor Hargreaves, and Herbert quickly follow Sylvia as she rushes down Frog Water Hill.

They see an elderly lady trying to push a shopping trolley up the hill.

The Teddies freeze. 'She has seen us,' whispers Sylvia. The lady's face lights up and she smiles.

'Teddies! Lovely teddies, I love Teddies. They are my favorite. Come here and live with me,' she says and she stoops down and picks up Herbert.

She pops Herbert on top of all her belongings in her shopping trolley and carefully places the other teddies neatly beside Herbert. The shopping trolley is full of clothes, blankets, newspapers and food.

'It smells a bit woofy in this trolley,' whispers Sir Victor Hargreaves.

'You mean poopy,' says Chit Chat.

'Smells of moldy food,' says Dusty.

'We are going the wrong way. The station is downhill,' whispers Herbert.

'We need to get out of here,' cries Sylvia. The trolley lady stops at the bus stop.

'A bus is coming,' says Sir Victor Hargreaves.

'How are we going to get to the Tower of London?' Herbert snaps.

'I have an idea,' says Sylvia 'when the bus stops, I suggest, on my say so, we jump out of this trolley and get on the bus.'

'But we will be seen,' Dusty replies.

'No, we won't. Just trust me,' says Sylvia.

The teddies can hear the bus stop, at the bus stop.

'Now, quick, let's jump out of the trolley,' says Sylvia.

The teddies jump and spring onto the bus and they hide under the seats. The door of the bus closes and moves on. A passenger in a pink coat calls out in a baby voice, 'Driver, come on, my Honey pops, drive faster. I want to get home to watch my program that starts at nine-thirty.'

'It is not my fault, Honeybunch. We got stuck in all that traffic going up Frog Water Hill,' the driver says.

'Don't bother picking anyone else up. Just drive quickly and let's get home.' She gets up, walks down the aisle, and sees the teddies. 'Careful, we have been seen,' says Chit Chat. 'The lady is coming this way and she is taking off her pink coat.'

The lady throws her pink coat on the seat by the teddies, and it slides onto the floor. 'What have we got here?' she asks, and her heavy dark eyebrows shoot up. She picks up Sir Victor Hargreaves.

'Alan, look, it's a bird baby,' the lady calls out to the driver. She purses her lips and kisses Sir Victor Hargreaves. The lady holds Sir Victor Hargreaves like a baby in her arms.

Chit Chat laughs. 'He won't like being called a bird baby. He likes to be called Sir Victor Hargreaves,' says Herbert.

‘He won’t like being kissed by a stranger,’ says Chit Chat.

‘It’s not funny, Chit Chat. How will we get Sir Victor Hargreaves back?’ Sylvia asks.

The lady in pink calls out, ‘My Honey pops, I’ve an idea. Forget tonight’s TV. Let us take this bus and get out of London. We could drive all night. We have a little bird baby to look after now.’

‘Yes, let’s do it!’ says the driver. ‘See how fast this bus can go,’ and he revs the engine.

TEN

THE RUNAWAY BUS.

The bus is driving fast now. Herbert climbs up onto the seat and looks out of the window.

'He's driving through red lights,' Herbert calls down to the others.

This makes the Teddies slide around the floor as the bus turns sharply around corners.

'I am feeling travel sick,' says Sylvia with her hands over her mouth.

'Me too,' replies Dusty.

'He is driving too fast,' says Chit Chat.

'Spell fast. F-A-S-T,' says the robotic voice of Herbert's Spell and Tell phone.

Herbert holds onto the seat. Police sirens wail. 'Come on, Honey pops. We don't want the police to catch up with us. Let's get out of here!'

the lady calls out, wiggling her arms and legs.

'I am not sure about this,' the bus driver says.

'Come on, don't slow down now!'

'My phone says we are heading towards London Bridge, the good news is this bus is number forty-three and it will take us to the Tower of London' says Herbert.

'That is good news, we should be able to get there on time,' says Dusty.

'My phone says the bus stops at Seven Sisters Road, Holloway Nags Head, Angel, Old Street, Moorgate, Great Swan Alley, Bank Station, Monument and London Bridge.'

'What's that about Great Swan Alley?' asks Sylvia.

'I would like to see a great swan, they're beautiful birds,' says Chit Chat.

'Chit Chat, will you stop thinking about swans and birds for one minute. What are we going to do?' asks Sylvia.

When the bus bounces over the bumps, it makes the Teddies roll some more on the floor. Red and blue lights flash, police cars sound their sirens.

'Pull over!' a policeman booms from a megaphone.

'We better stop, for the police. Let me do the talking,' says the lady as she stuffs Sir Victor Hargreaves under her jumper.

The bus screeches to a halt and, as the bus slows down, all the teddies slide to one side.

Sir Victor Hargreaves pushes himself out of her jumper with his beak and he finds her pink fluffy coat on the floor, he hides under it.

'Come on everyone, hide under the coat as well,' Sylvia suggests.

The front door of the bus opens, and several police officers enter the bus. The Teddies are in the darkness hiding under the coat and hear footsteps. Someone is coming down the steps.

'What is going on here?' shouts a male

passenger. 'I was sitting upstairs on the top deck fast asleep, and I missed my stop.'

Sylvia peeps out from under the coat. 'Look, it's our next-door neighbor, the headmaster,' says Sylvia.

'Who is responsible for this chaos? I have never been on a bus that brakes so sharply and drives at such speed. It is a disgrace,' calls the headmaster in a loud voice.

'The headmaster! It's Mr. Mason from our old school,' says the driver.

'Jade Parker and Alan Wallis, I should have known you two would have had something to do with it. I remember you both from School. How could I forget? I cannot go anywhere without bumping into old pupils from my school. Can I just remind you that I am the headmaster of one of the biggest schools in London – Frog Water Academy – and you, if I'm correct, are former pupils from that very school? But I have never in all my life experienced such driving.

You are a disgrace to the purple school blazers that you used to wear. I will need to see both of you in my office or should I say upstairs on the top deck,' cries out Mr. Mason the headmaster.

'Sorry, Sir, but my name is Jade Wallis now. Alan and I got married last summer,' says the lady in pink.

'Sorry, Jade Wallis, but my wedding invitation must have got lost in the post,' says the headmaster.

'We did not invite you. It was a very small wedding,' says Alan.

'I'm joking,' says the headmaster.

'Mr. Mason, do you remember me?' asks a police officer with ginger hair who was also climbing aboard the bus.

'Robin Brentwood, of course I remember you. Hands always in your pockets, slouching. Always missing choir practice, yes, you better come up and see me as well,' he says and he turns and goes upstairs to the top deck.

Robin the Police officer says, 'Perhaps we should all go upstairs to the top deck and have a little chat about what has just happened.'

Jade and Alan go up the stairs followed by the two police officers.

'They have gone upstairs. Come on. Let's grab the chance to get off the bus,' says Sylvia as she holds onto the coat to cover them as the teddies jump off.

ELEVEN

THE TOWER OF LONDON.

The teddies holding onto the pink furry coat scurry down the street. 'I can't see where I am going,' Dusty says, tripping over her own paws.

'Keep moving,' says Herbert from the front of the coat.

'You are treading on my feet, bird baby,' giggles Chit Chat.

'I cannot believe she was calling me a bird baby. Why, I am Sir Victor Hargreaves,' says Sir Victor Hargreaves.

Herbert stops suddenly and the other teddies crash into him. Herbert peers out from beneath the coat to look at the street. In front of them shining in the bright lights is the Tower of London.

'Come on, we need to keep walking,' Sylvia orders.

'It is a long way to walk, my feet hurt,' complains Chit Chat.

The teddies stop and take a rest.

Herbert lifts the coat and he sees across the lawn, the Tower of London.

'It looks incredible – what a sight,' Dusty says with a big smile.

'Come on, we have no time to wait,' Sylvia commands the other teddies, she throws down the coat and runs across the lawn towards the Tower of London. The other Teddies run after her.

'Queen Sylvia, Sylvia, stop. Someone will see you!' yells Sir Victor Hargreaves as he runs after her.

Sylvia stops when she gets close to the wall of the Tower of London, all the Teddies stand close to her.

‘How will we get in?’ Sylvia asks the others.

‘Let’s follow a group of people. I will form a dust ball and we will move in the shadows,’ suggests Dusty, pointing to a group of people who are having a night tour of the Tower of London.

Sylvia nods in agreement and Dusty claps her paws together and swirls them around. Dust fills the air. The Teddies draw close to Dusty as they move softly behind the small group of people.

A tour guide holds an umbrella and talks to the group of tourists. ‘You are in for a treat tonight, a special tour of the tower. You will see the famous ceremony of the keys at seven minutes to ten o’clock. You will see the Chief Yeoman Warder walk this way. He carries in one hand a lantern and in the other hand the King’s keys. He will meet the guard over there.’ The tour guide points with his umbrella to where the Yeoman Warder will walk and where in a moment he will meet the guards.'

As the tour group moves away, Dusty dust falls to the ground to reveal the teddies standing in a small circle. The Teddies cough. 'The keys are guarded by soldiers; we are never going to get the key to Make believe,' says Herbert.

'We need a plan,' Sir Victor Hargreaves says.

'Yes, a plan,' Sylvia says as she rubs her paw with her chin. 'We need to think of a plan.'

'I am thinking but I can't think of anything,' says Dusty.

'No wonder the key to Make believe is here, with all the guards. It is impossible. We might as well give up,' grumbles Herbert.

'We can't give up, Herbert. I will speak to the ravens and ask them to help us,' Chit Chat says. Chit Chat strides up to the two ravens that are on the courtyard. He bends down to whisper to one of the ravens and the raven squawks loudly in his ear.

‘I don’t think they understand me,’ says Chit Chat.

‘Of course they cannot understand you, Chit Chat. Let me speak to them. I am an Eagle,’ says Sir Victor Hargreaves.

Sir Victor Hargreaves walks up to the raven. ‘Excuse me, Mr. Raven, my name is Sir Victor Hargreaves,’ and he gives a bow.

The raven squawks loudly at Sir Victor Hargreaves.

‘How rude!’ says Sir Victor Hargreaves.

‘Look, he’s coming,’ declares Herbert.

‘Who?’ Dusty asks.

‘The Chief Yeoman Warder, he’s coming this way,’ Chit Chat shouts.

‘He is on his own. We must get the keys off him now before he meets the other guards,’ Sylvia announces.

‘But we don’t have a plan,’ says Chit Chat.

The Chief Yeoman Warder marches towards the teddies. Holding in one hand was a lantern and in the other hand were the keys.

'I am going to get the key,' says Dusty. 'Come on, Sylvia. I am going to form a dust ball and together we will roll towards the Chief Yeoman Warder.'

'I can't look,' says Sylvia as she holds on to Dusty.

The dust ball rolls closer to the Chief Yeoman Warder, then with a plop bumps into him. He stumbles and drops the lantern. Sylvia grabs the keys out of his hand. The dust ball continues to roll. Sylvia and Dusty collapse on the ground with Sylvia holding onto the keys. She grabs hold of the gold key with the butter glow bird engraved on it and holds the key close to her chest. Then two gold butter glow birds fly towards her, the birds swoop down and start pecking and biting at Sylvia. The butter glow bird pulls blue stuffing out of the hole in Sylvia's chest. The blue stuffing flies into the air.

'Get off of me!' Sylvia cries out.

TWELVE

REMEMBER ME, LIKE I REMEMBER YOU.

The butter glow birds try to pull the keys from Sylvia's paws, but she won't let go. Just then, four ravens fly above Sylvia squawking at the butter glow birds. That makes Sylvia drop the keys and one of the ravens picks the keys up in her beak and flies off. The raven lands near the Chief Yeoman Warder and drops the keys on the ground. The Chief Yeoman Warder picks up the lantern and the keys. The butter glow birds fly away from the tower with two of the ravens flying after them.

The Chief Yeoman Warder walks towards the Tower. 'I must get the key,' Sylvia pants, feeling weak as she lifts herself up and chases after the Chief Yeoman Warder.

The Chief Yeoman Warder marches towards the other soldiers. The soldiers are calling out to one and another. The Chief Yeoman Warder then marches behind a door in the Tower and the door is shut. Sylvia can hear the clanging sound of the door being locked and she falls to the ground, completely exhausted. 'It is too late,' she cries, covering her one eye with her paw. The other teddies rush to comfort her.

'You have lost a lot of stuffing, my sister,' says Dusty.

'Quick, put all the stuffing back in her; she is very weak,' says Sir Victor Hargreaves.

The blue stuffing is scattered across the ground and the teddies run about to collect it all.

Sir Victor Hargreaves pushes the stuffing back into the gap in Sylvia's chest.

'I have collected as much as I can,' says Chit Chat, holding onto the blue stuffing and passing it to Sir Victor Hargreaves,

Sylvia coughs.

'There is not enough stuffing. Those butter glow birds have flown off with it,' exclaims Sir Victor Hargreaves.

Dusty tries to tear a hole in her own chest.

'What are you doing?' Sir Victor Hargreaves asks Dusty.

'Sylvia can have some of my stuffing. I just need to tear a hole in my chest and get some of my stuffing out,' Dusty replies. She removes a little bit of stuffing and puts it in Sylvia's hole in her chest.

'Are you sure about this?' asks Sir Victor Hargreaves.

'Yes, it is fine. She needs it more than me,' replies Dusty.

Sylvia slowly sits up.

'Your Majesty are you feeling stronger?' bellows Sir Victor Hargreaves.

'Thank you, thank you, Dusty, my sister, for

giving me some of your stuffing,' Sylvia says weakly.

'Those butter glows came from Teddy Land. They stopped us getting the key,' Herbert cries.

'It's too late. We have not been able to get the key. I will never be able to get the key to make believe and bring it back to Teddy Bear Mountain; It is the end. Children will never play Teddy Land again!' Sylvia sobs.

'This is a sad day,' Dusty says wiping a tear from her eye.

Herbert cries, 'Our children, Emma and Tyler, will forget all about us and how they used to play Teddy Land.'

'Look at that full moon. This is the last time children will sleep and remember Teddy Land. When they wake up they will have forgotten all about Teddy Land and the Teddies they used to play with. They will never play with us again,' Sylvia continues to sob. She gets up and walks along the path. The moon shines brightly in the sky and Sylvia can see the reflection of the moon in a puddle on the ground.

'I like playing Teddy Land with you in the moonlight,' whispers Sylvia. Sylvia dips her paw in the puddle and swirls the water around. In the Puddle, Sylvia imagines seeing Emma and Tyler Miller playing with their teddies in Teddy land.

'Will you remember me, like I remember you?' Sylvia sings.

Do you remember how we used to play Teddy Land?

'remember me, like I remember you, like you remember me,

like I remember you.

When I am out of sight, playing in the moonlight,

Remember me, like I remember you.

Will you remember how we used to play Teddy Land?

Oh, Teddy Land, oh Teddy Land,

Will you try to forget as if we never met?
Will you remember how we used to play Teddy Land?

I know you will always remember me,

Playing in the moonlight.

Teddy Land. Oh, Teddy Land.

Of course, I remember playing Teddy Land.

Teddy Land. I remember Teddy Land, like I remember you,

Like you remember me.

I remember how we used to play Teddy land.

It was a game of Make believe.

Emma and Tyler, sister, and brother,

I remember your laughter.'

'For I remember you, like you remember me,' Dusty sings back to Sylvia. Dusty holds onto Sylvia's paw, and they dance together in the moonlight.

Sylvia puts a hand on her chest and sings.

The Teddies all sing together.

'They will always remember Teddy Land.

When our children grow up, they will remember Teddy Land.

Teddy Land, oh Teddy Land—'

Sylvia suddenly stops singing and feels something sharp under the fur in her chest. In the moonlight a gold light is shining from inside Sylvia. 'What is that under your fur?' Dusty asks. Sylvia looks down at her chest and under her stuffing she can see something glistening. She feels with her paws.

'Maybe a small stone,' Sylvia said out loud.

Sylvia pulls out something gold from her chest. Not a stone at all but a small, gold key. 'It's the key,' cries Sylvia.

'It's the key. We found it,' shouts Dusty jumping up and down.

'I had the key to Make believe inside me all this time,' says Sylvia.

'It was hidden inside you the whole time,' Sir Victor Hargreaves calls out as he rushes over to Sylvia.

'Or maybe it was hidden in you, Dusty, and you gave it to me when you gave me some of your stuffing,' Sylvia says to Dusty.

'I guess we will never know,' replies Dusty, laughing.

'It doesn't matter how you got it. We have the key,' Herbert says excitedly, jumping up and down in the puddle.

'We have the key!' shouts Chit Chat.

'Come on, let's get back to Teddy Land, I have the key, the key to Make believe was in me.' says Sylvia clasping her paws together with joy.

THIRTEEN
THE SUITCASE HOPPERS.

Herbert looks up the map on his phone. 'We have to go over the bridge,' says Herbert.

'We are going in the wrong direction,' says Sir Victor Hargreaves. 'We need to be going north, not south. We need to get back to Highgate.' Sir Victor Hargreaves peers down at the river below the bridge.

'I am just following what it says on my phone,' answers Herbert.

'Your phone is wrong,' says Sir Victor Hargreaves.

'See that man,' says Chit Chat. 'He is getting a Taxi. Let's hop into his suitcase and travel with him, I am a suitcase hopper, I travel all the time in suitcases, follow me. I will get us home. Chit Chat and Dusty walk up quietly behind the man, and they unzip his suitcase. Dusty climbs into the case, the other teddies climb in after her. Sir Victor Hargreaves is the last teddy to get into the suitcase. Sir Victor Hargreaves's beak sticks out and he uses one eye to peer out of the suitcase.

'Where to?' asks the driver.

'City airport,' replies the young man, and he lifts the suitcase and puts it in the taxi and then the man sits down in the cab with his suitcase close to his feet.

The man sighs as his mobile phone rings. He answers his phone.

'Yes...I am on the way to the airport...I am so tired...' he says.

'This is so exciting, we are going to the airport,' whispers Dusty.

'We want to get back home to Frog Water Hill,' says Sylvia.

'The man with the suitcase is falling asleep,' says Sir Victor Hargreaves.

'The driver is listening to his radio.'

'Brilliant! The man is asleep!' exclaims Sylvia. 'Sir Victor Hargreaves, speak in a load voice and give directions to the driver.'

'Change of plan, driver. Can you drop me off at Frog Water Hill?' says Sir Victor Hargreaves in a loud voice.

'Frog Water Hill? I thought you wanted the airport,' says the driver.

'Never mind that, Frog Water Hill, please,' Sir Victor Hargreaves replies.

'Well, make up your mind. What's the address?' asks the driver.

'The Old School House, Frog Water Hill, Highgate. Do you know it?' asks Sir Victor Hargreaves.

'Do I know Frog Water Hill? Of course, I know it. I went to the school on Frog Water Hill. Frog Water Academy. I nearly became head boy, but they gave it to Simon Moley instead. Does someone in your family work at the school? To live in Frog Water Hill your family must have some connection to the school. Don't tell me you're related to Mr. Mason. He was my headmaster when I went to the school. Are your family teachers?'

'Yes. Emma and Tyler Miller. Their mum and dad are teachers at the school,' says Sir Victor Hargreaves.

Sylvia pulls Sir Victor Hargreaves' wing.

'Sir Victor Hargreaves, why did you say that? Stop talking!' demands Sylvia.

'Miller? Yes, I have heard the name.'

'He needs to stop talking,' Dusty whispers to Sylvia.

'I think the headmaster Mr. Mason lives in the next house. You would not want to mess with him,' says the driver.

'What do I say?' whispers Sir Victor Hargreaves.

'Say nothing,' replies Sylvia.

'I know Mr. Mason,' Sir Victor Hargreaves says quickly.

'I told you not to say anything,' whispers

Sylvia.

'Lots of famous people have gone to Frog Water Academy,' continues the driver.

'He is still talking to us,' says Herbert.

'Sir Victor Hargreaves don't say anything more,' orders Sylvia. 'He cannot find out that he has been talking to a teddy.'

'Did you hear me back there? Okay, don't talk to me then. Just ignore me. Mr Snooty,' says the driver to himself under his breath.

'My name is not Mr. Snooty. It is Sir Victor Hargreaves to you.'

'Well, excuse me, Sir Victor Hargreaves,' says the Driver. The taxi driver swings the taxi round the corner, so the suitcase slides around.

Chit Chat shakes his head and says 'You have gone and upset him. Taxi drivers are like scarecrows—they like to have a chit-chat. He may not take us to Frog Water Hill now. Let me chat with him. I know how to chat,'

'Nobody else is going to speak to him,' says Sylvia.

‘But I have the chat. Please, please let me talk to him,’ pleads Chit Chat.

‘No, you are not chatting with him. We will sit here in silence,’ says Sylvia quietly.

Chit Chat frowns and folds his arms. The Teddies are silent for the rest of the journey.

The taxi pulls up outside of Emma and Tyler’s house.

‘Here we are, the old school house, Frog Water Hill,’ says the driver.

The passenger in the back seat wakes up. ‘This is not the airport, why have you brought me here?’ the man says in a sleepy voice.

‘You said Frog Water Hill.’

‘I did not,’ the man retorts.

The taxi driver gets out of his cab in a huff.

‘Get out of my cab! Sir Victor Hargreaves or whatever your name is!’ he shouts and pulls the man out of his cab by his jacket.

‘My suitcase!’ says the man.

The suitcase is still in the taxi.

'Listen here, Sir Victor Hargreaves,' says the driver.

'Who is Sir Victor Hargreaves? I am not Sir Victor Hargreaves. I asked you to take me to the airport. I am going to miss my flight,' complains the man.

A police car pulls up and out steps Robin Brentwood the police officer and the headmaster, Mr. Mason.

'Thank you, Robin Brentwood, for dropping me home. What a terrible business on the bus this evening,' says the headmaster to the policeman.

The taxi driver shouts, 'You told me that your name was Sir Victor Hargreaves and that you wanted to be dropped off here and not the airport.'

Mr. Mason hears the taxi man shouting.

'What's going on here? Another old student from Frog Water Academy,' says Mr. Mason as he looks at the driver. 'Stanley Jones! Why are you shouting in the street?'

'Sorry, Headmaster, I was just driving this man to the airport and then he said he wanted to be dropped off at The Old School House,' Stanley says.

'I wanted the airport,' says the man.

'Jones,' says Mr. Mason, 'take this man to the airport and stop shouting in the street. You're a disgrace to your old school blazer that you used to wear and to think I nearly made you head boy of Frog Water Academy instead of Simon Moley.'

Sir Victor Hargreaves unzips the suitcase and whispers, 'Come on, they are not looking, let's go.'

FOURTEEN

QUEEN SYLVIA IS BACK IN TEDDY LAND.

Sylvia is back in Teddy Land running through Bluebell wood. Sir Victor Hargreaves flies above in the sky, Herbert, Dusty, and Chit Chat sprints down the path. When Sylvia reaches the wishing gate, She rests against it.

'I can't run anymore,' says Dusty as she flops down on the ground.

'We have to go to my cave,' says Sylvia. 'From there I know an underground tunnel that will leads us to Teddy Bear Mountain.'

They all climb over the wishing gate, walk along the path, and finally get to Sylvia's cave. Then they crawl into the cave.

'Who goes there?' calls a voice from the

darkness.

'Sylvia and this is my cave! Who are you?'

'It's us, Merton and Bella.'

The Dragon and the Monkey step forward.

'We have been waiting for you. We know you have the found the key to make believe,' says Merton.

'Yes, we have it,' says Sylvia.

'This must be your long-lost sister Dusty and Chit Chat,' says Bella.

`Yes, how did you know?' asks Sylvia.

'We've been watching you with Zomba magic. You need to enter Teddy Bear Mountain quickly and find the door to Make Believe,' Merton tells Sylvia.

'What about the dragons? What about Narodoon?' asks Herbert.

'The Queen of Teddy Land knows how to use the tunnel to get inside the mountain. I will see to Narodoon. Do not worry about that,' replies Merton.

‘Come on!’ commands Sylvia, and she walks on. ‘Herbert. Can you shine your torch, so I can see,’ says Sylvia. ‘Here it is,’ she says and she pushes the wall with her paws.

Slowly the wall moves to the side revealing a flight of steps.

‘Dusty and Herbert you come with me, Chit Chat, Sir Victor Hargreaves, stay behind and guard the tunnel,’ says Sylvia.

‘Stay here? I want to hide. I don’t want to fight dragons. They will rip me apart,’ says Chit Chat.

‘You will be okay to fight them. I have magical zomba swords for you,’ replies Bella.

Bella claps her hands and no sooner the sound rings out several magical zomba swords appear. Sir Victor Hargreaves picks up a sword. ‘I am ready for the dragons.’

Suddenly there is a loud hissing and swishing sound.

‘It’s the dragons. They have found us,’

shrieks Chit Chat.

A deep voice echoes through the cave. 'Merton, we know you are in the cave. We have come to get the Book of Zomba,' bellows King Rotter.

'Stay away do not enter the cave,' calls out Merton 'I will never give up the Book of Zomba.'

'Then come out here and face us,' answers King Rotter.

Quickly, Sylvia, Dusty, and Herbert rush down the steps to reach Teddy Bear Mountain.

Merton says, 'They have gone! Quickly hide the tunnel and I will go out and face King Rotter.'

Merton leaps out of the cave and flies at King Rotter. Both dragons rise into the air. Flapping their wings, spitting out fire.

King Rotter flies higher and higher above dragon Merton. King Rotter shoots out his large claws and grabbing Merton by the tail.

Merton breaks free from King Rotter and soars higher into the sky, blowing fire down on King Rotter.

'They are fighting with fire,' yells Sir Victor Hargreaves.

'Let's use our water swords. We can spray the Dragons with water,' says Bella as she waves her sword in the air.

Sir Victor Hargreaves flies into the air brandishing his sword and spraying water at King Rotter and his dragons.

'I am not afraid of dragons,' calls out Chit Chat as he joins the battle.

FIFTEEN

THE SPELL ON FRED'S SHOES.

Meanwhile, Sylvia crawls along the tunnel until she comes up to a large rock.

'This is it. I just must push this rock aside so we may enter Teddy Bear Mountain,' says Sylvia. Sylvia and Dusty push the rock while Herbert shines the torch from his phone. Dust from the roof of the tunnel falls onto his head.

Sylvia pushes with all her strength and slowly the rock moves. There before them, they see a large sparkling rock pool with silver reeds and butter glow birds flying overhead.

'We've done it, come on,' says Sylvia excitedly.

'What's over there?' says Dusty.

Sylvia, Dusty, and Herbert jump from rock

to rock.

'It's Fred's trainer,' says Herbert and he goes to picks them up.

Herbert holds the trainers in his hands. The trainers turn from red to gold and then into two gold Butter glow birds. The birds peck at Herbert's paws before they fly away. Herbert licks his paws.

'The dragons have put a spell on Fred's shoes,' says Dusty.

'We have found his trainer but where's my brother?' asks Herbert.

'Fred!' yells Sylvia

'We are here, we are here,' calls back a voice.

The Teddies look around in amazement.

`Come on, I can hear them this way,' says Dusty, and she rushes on and the others follow.

They turn a corner and there they see Fred tied to a rock and the Hippos, Walter, Angela, Pinkie, Scarecrowie, and Chesney the hobby horse strapped together.

‘Fred?’ yells Sylvia. As quickly as they can Sylvia, Dusty, and Herbert run over to Fred. Sylvia unties Fred. Herbert releases the Hippos. Dusty frees Chesney the Hobby horse and Scarecrowie. Sylvia gives Fred a big hug.

At that moment three butter glow birds fly overhead carrying gold scissors. They duck their heads to avoid the danger of the flying scissors. The scissors snip at Chesney the hobby horse’s mane.

‘My mane! It’s cutting my mane. I am getting out of here,’ cries Chesney, and he gallops out of the cave. The scissors follow him, snipping at him as he jumps.

‘Fred, this is our long-lost sister Dusty, I met her in the attic,’ says Sylvia.

‘Hello, my brother,’ says Dusty as she hugs Fred and her dust fills the air. Fred coughs.

‘Have you seen a door?’ asks Sylvia. ‘I need to find the door to Make believe.’

‘Over, there is a gold door, near the gold

bush,' replies Fred.

Sylvia runs to the door. She brushes aside the butter glow birds who are flying about. She hears Sir Victor Hargreaves calling her as he flies at them from the tunnel on the other side.

'Your majesty,' he squawks.

Sylvia turns around. 'What is happening Sir Victor Hargreaves?'

'Your majesty, you do not have much time. The mountain is crumbling. You need to escape, or you will be trapped here forever. We must leave now.'

'No, I am not ready to go yet. I want to go through the gold door first,' Sylvia announces.

SIXTEEN
MAKE BELIEVE.

The Teddies stand quite still. What is going to happen? Sylvia turns the key. Slowly the door opens and reveals a magical land of Make believe. There before them is a rippling river and sparkling waterfalls and singing mermaids perched on rocks.

A rowing boat glides gently towards the teddies.

Sylvia yawns and stretches her arms above her head, then she carefully climbs into the rowing boat.

The Mermaid sings 'Come along teddies, to see all the Teddy Lands in the world. Imagine it. Make believe it and you can see it.'

The teddies jump into the boat; Fred sits

next to Sylvia.

'I feel sleepy,' yawns Fred.

The boat floats along the stream.

'Look! Unicorns!' Dusty calls out.

The boat floats past weeping willows, unicorns jump on the banks of the river. Pixies and fairies fly high in the sky.

'I can see a little elf,' says the pink hippo, Pinkie pointing to an elf sitting on a flower.

'You will see it if you imagine it,' sings the Mermaid.

They float past a gingerbread house. 'That house looks tasty,' says Walter the hippo, licking his lips.

The boat floats past a giant who is sitting in a field. He puts his giant hand in the river and makes giant waves making the boat rise into the sky and then land in the river again.

'Whoa!' shrieks Kim the silver hippo.

'The boat is heading towards a waterfall,' Angela the Hippo shouts out.

It is then too late! The boat hurdles over the waterfall. The teddies get wet. The boat lands in the water below with a crash and then starts to spin.

'What fun,' cries Pinkie the Hippo.

Bubbles from the river float up to the sky and slowly the boat slows down.

Dark shadows gather as they pass through a dark wood.

A witch with a long black cloak sits on a tree branch. She smiles as they float past. 'I don't like this part of the river.' Kim the Hippo says in a trembling voice.

'All this is Make believe,' Sylvia says.

'Look, I can see a dinosaur,' Angela says, pointing to a dinosaur.

The lake turns to ice, and the teddies see snowmen ice-skating in a circle. Suddenly the ice cracks and the boat moves quickly down the flowing river towards some more rapids.

'There's another waterfall!' warns Dusty.

The boat rises.

'We're flying!' exclaims Fred.

'Yes, we are flying,' repeats Sylvia.

'I can't believe what is happening,' says Fred. 'This is my dream come true. I've always wanted to fly. I am flying here with my brother and sisters.' Then the boat flies higher and higher into space. 'Look at the planets and all the stars,' Sir Victor Hargreaves calls out.

Pillows fly past them with teddies sitting on them.

'What are those? They look like giant pillows with teddies on them,' marvels Dusty.

'Don't you see? It's different Teddy Lands. All the different Teddy Lands in the world. Floating up here in space,' Sylvia says.

Then a family of Teddies sitting on a pillow floats past. Sylvia calls out to an orange bear sitting on a pillow next to a fluffy pink cat, 'Excuse me. I am looking for our Teddy Land. I am looking for Emma and Tyler Miller's Teddy

Land.'

'Sorry, we belong to Ghita,' responds the orange bear.

'Look, it's King Rotter,' says Kim the Hippo.

'He's asleep on that pillow,' says Pinkie.

A blue pillow flies closer to the boat with the blue dragon fast asleep with other dragons beside him. King Rotter opens his eyes and sits up.

'Queen Sylvia!' calls out King Rotter. 'The Children love playing Dragon Land and playing with me.'

'But they always loved dragons,' says Sylvia.

'My children love dragons, They have dragon wallpaper, dragon bedding,' says King Rotter

'Don't forget the dragon lunch boxes,' says Yella, the yellow dragon who has also woken up.

The boat starts to fly lower.

'What about Narodoon?' calls out Sylvia

'What did you say?' calls back King Rotter.

'Narodoon, Narodoooon.'

'We are going down, doon' announces Fred.

Slowly the boat sinks and lands in a rough sea. As the waves rise up and down, this causes the teddies to slide about in the boat. The mermaids swim alongside to steady the boat singing a song to calm the waters.

'Make believe, all the Teddy Lands in all the world,' the mermaids sing.

One of the mermaids jumps into the boat. She has long, white hair. She picks up Sylvia and kisses her on the head.

'Sylvia, this is your world, my teddy bear. The moon and the stars are all here for you. Remember me, like I remember you, oh Teddy Land, play Teddy Land, My Teddy bear, play Teddy Land. For I remember you, like you remember me. Let's play Teddy Land, oh Teddy Land, My Teddy bear, play Teddy Land,' sings the Mermaid.

Then the boat floats towards a rock situated in the middle of the sea. The Teddies lean over the boat. Sylvia points ahead.

'Look there on the rock, it's the golden door. The door back to our Teddy Land,' shouts Sylvia.

When they reach the rock, the mermaid helps them to climb out of the boat. One by one they climb up the rock. The gold door opens and there they see their own dear Teddy Land. The Teddies go through the door when they see where they are, and they shout out,

'We're back in Teddy Land! There's my palace, There is the mud pool,' cries Sylvia.

'There is Teddy Bear Mountain,' says Herbert.

Merton the dragon is standing with his daughter Bella on a craggy rock by the side of the mud pool. The green dragon spreads out his wings.

'We did it, Merton, and we went through the door to Make believe. We got to see all the Teddy Lands in the world. There are hundreds of them, all of them behind the door. So many children have Teddy Lands. They have their favorite Teddies in Teddy Land. They have not forgotten Teddy Land. Children still play Teddy Land all over the world,' Sylvia tells Merton.

'You went behind the door?' croaks Merton.

'Yes, yes. Thank you for helping us to save Teddy Land. I invite you, Merton and Bella, to stay here in Teddy Land forever,' Sylvia offers.

'Yes, thank you. We will stay here,' Merton says.

Sylvia gazes at the mountain. 'All the rocks have returned to the mountain,' says Merton.

'Your Majesty the mountain is safe. It is not crumbling anymore,' says Sir Victor Hargreaves.

'Apple Crumble?' asks Pinkie

'Don't start that crumble business again,' says Sir Victor Hargreaves.

There is a sound of heavy footsteps, coming from Bluebell Woods.

'It's Narodoon,' Fred yells to Sylvia.

Narodoon lowers her head and begins to close her eyes.

'Queen Sylvia, I don't want to sleep all the time in the mountain. I want to be able to come out and play in Teddy Land. I want to swim in lakes and mud pools,' Narodoon yawns.

'Then don't go back inside the mountain,' says Sylvia 'Stay here and have fun with us.'

`You don't understand. I am the monster of the mountain. I must protect the door of Make believe,' says Narodoon.

`But you can still protect the mountain and be out and about in Teddy Land,' says Merton.

`You can?' asks Narodoon and her eyes light up.

'Yes, with a little bit of Zomba magic from the Book of Zomba. I still have the Book of Zomba.'

'Then I will stay in Teddy Land. King Rotter wanted me to destroy Teddy Land. I think King Rotter had me under a spell. I was not myself. Forgive me,' says Narodoon.

'He did have you under a spell. He put a spell on you when he woke you up, but the spell is broken now. He has no power over you anymore,' says Merton.

'King Rotter is a Rotter. I want to have fun and play in Teddy Land. I am pleased you saved Teddy Land and stopped my mountain from crumbling,' says Narodoon.

'King Rotter wants everyone to believe he is rotten to the core but deep down he is a sweet dragon. He wants to play his rotten games,' says Merton.

'Papa, I don't trust King Rotter.' whispers Bella.

'Bella, my dear. King Rotter is not to be feared. He just wants to be loved and he has found that children love dragons as well as teddies,' interrupts Merton.

'Yes, we found King Rotter in the Land of Make Believe. He says that children love dragons and love to play dragon land. I am not frightened of King Rotter and his rotten games,' says Sylvia.

Sir Victor Hargreaves announces, 'Queen Sylvia saved Teddy Land and found the key to Make believe. We must celebrate.'

'Thank you, Sir Victor Hargreaves. I did it with the help of all of you,' says Sylvia with a big smile spread across her face.

Chit Chat and Chester the hobby horse gallop down the path. Scarecrowie hugs his brother, Chit Chat.

'We are all together again, playing Teddy Land. Let's sing a song,' says Scarecrowie.

'Let's sing the Rocking Horse Rock,' sings Chester the Hobby horse.

The Teddies dance in a circle and sing. The Hippos dive into the mud pool and Walter plays his tin whistle.

'Let's dance the Boogie!' cries Sir Victor Hargreaves as he flaps his wings and bends his knees.

'Look, Fred, everyone is playing in Teddy Land. Join in the dance with us,' says Sylvia as she leads Fred into the circle. In the middle of the circle is Merton the dragon, Queen Sylvia climbs onto the dragon's back and the dragon runs out of the circle and flies into the sky. Queen Sylvia looks down on Teddy land as she clings onto the dragons.

'I have looked at Teddy Land from so many different ways, I have looked high, I have looked low and I have found Teddy Land in me. I have found Teddy Land in you. Only today, I look at Teddy Land this way,' says Queen Sylvia.

THE END

ABOUT THE AUTHOR.

Esther Duggan lives in North London. She remembers playing Teddy Land with her brother Jerry.
Esther did a stand-up comedy course in 2023 and performed her show-case at the Backyard comedy club.

Teddy Land is her first novel.

A message from Esther Duggan author.

Building a relationship with my readers is very important to me. You can find out more about Teddy Land and my books on my social media.

Just Visit:
Tik Tok   Esther Duggan author
esther dugganauthor@esther story teller

Tik Tok Estherstoryteller.
Instagram Esther Duggan author
Facebook Esther Duggan author

For more information visit my Link Tree profile on https://linktre.ee/estherdugganauthor

Teddy Land is my first book, please spread the word so other readers can discover Teddy Land and if you have enjoyed the book, please leave me a review on social media. Thank you

A BIG THANK YOU.

My Mum, Lauren, DK, Kate, MS, KH, Steven, Writers group, Joanna, Sarah, Louisa, Dad, Judith, Daniel and Family.